On the Far Side of the Mirror

by
B. B. Hiller and Neil W. Hiller

illustrated by
Jody Lee

SCHOLASTIC INC.
New York Toronto London Auckland Sydney

For our sisters, Gwen, Judy, Molly, and Penny,
who also appear *de temps en temps*.

ISBN 0-590-33683-5

12 11 10 9 8 7 6 5 4 3 2 1   1   6 7 8 9/8 0 1/9

Printed in the U.S.A.   28

Before you read this story, you should know there is something special about it. In the story, two cousins solve a mystery that has puzzled their family for generations. But there is also a second mystery woven into the story that *you* can solve.

More than thirty clues to the second mystery appear in the story. You are looking for a very large object. It's bright, it's long, it's cold. Now you see it, later you won't. Here is another clue: The object you are searching for is never mentioned.

If you haven't solved the second mystery by the time you get to the end of the story, you'll get a second chance. But don't look at the back of the book now! Wait, please!

Table of Contents

Monkey Business

"... and she has a monkey named Sherlock," Ted's mother said, while she served lunch. "Cindy will be bringing him here to visit, too."

Ted groaned, running his fingers through his curly brown hair. "Oh, Mom. Come on!" What a way to kill a guy's vacation! How could he ever explain *this* to his friends? His father interrupted sharply.

"Ted!" Ted glanced at his dad. The look on the man's face was Trouble. Ted decided to keep his thoughts to himself. He hoped his goofy cousin's monkey didn't have a tin cup, too. At least she was only visiting Finlay for two weeks.

Ted furrowed his brow over bright blue eyes. The expression on his summer-tanned face seemed to show that he was uneasy about his cousin's visit. Yet around his mouth now, as frequently, there was the ghost of a grin, as if he looked forward to the very thing that worried him.

Ted's mother babbled on about Cindy's visit. Cindy had lived all over the world. That's why Ted had never met her before. "But you'll know her right away. Remember Cindy's picture on their Christmas card last year?" Ted shook his head. "Well, she's a strawberry blond with freckles. In fact, Cindy looks just like Great-Granny Morehouse in the oval picture hanging in the recreation room. My sister Penny gave her Great-Granny Morehouse's locket, too. Funny thing about that locket. . . ."

His mother often talked about "that locket." Ted had heard the story many times before. It wasn't the strange green stone on the *outside* of the locket that puzzled the family. It was the color photograph of Great-Granny Morehouse on the *inside.* The picture of her as an adult was already inside, so the family story went, when she got the locket in 1910. She was then about Ted's — and Cindy's — age.

But Great-Granny Morehouse had never said exactly where she got the locket with the mysterious picture — a puzzle handed down with the locket, through generations of Ted's family.

And now his cousin Cindy was coming on the afternoon train, bringing her monkey, Sherlock, and the locket, with her.

Ted's mother continued, ". . . So we never will know the story behind that locket — "

Interrupting herself, she looked up at the clock on the wall.

"Ted, it's time for you to go to the station to meet Cindy. Hurry now."

Ted didn't mind the walk to the Finlay train station. It gave him a chance to think about what his mother had said. He was curious to see the legendary locket. Maybe it was really valuable.

Ted got to the station just before the train pulled in. He watched the people getting off. First there was a man in a soldier's uniform. About twenty people were waiting for him. Next came a tall man with piercing eyes and a small, square mustache, wearing a black top hat and a flowing cape. He carried many boxes and bags, as well as a cage full of doves. Ted stared as the man passed. The man seemed to see straight through Ted. Ted turned back to the train.

Then he saw a girl about his own age. A monkey eating popcorn was perched on her shoulder. Definitely Cindy. She does look like the picture of Great-grandmother in the rec room, Ted thought, noticing the irrepressible smile and bright green eyes that dominated her face. Cindy had a suitcase in each hand. Ted walked up to her.

"Cindy?" She nodded. "I'm Ted. Here, let me help you."

"Hi, Ted. This is Sherlock," she said, handing Ted a suitcase. To Ted's surprise, the monkey stuck out his small right hand for him to shake. Solemnly, Ted shook hands with Sherlock. Then Ted felt silly and dropped the little hand.

"Come on," he said, picking up one of Cindy's suitcases. "My mom's waiting for us."

They turned to walk out of the station.

"On, no!" Cindy cried, suddenly. "My astronomy handbook! I left it on the train. Sherlock! Go get it!"

Sherlock stuck the popcorn box in Ted's hand, then he leaped from Cindy's shoulder and grabbed onto one of the station's overhead beams. Swiftly, he swung from one beam to the next until he reached the edge of the platform. Then, swinging into the door of the train car, he disappeared from the cousins' view.

Suddenly the whistle blew, the conductor shouted, "ALL ABOARD!" and the train began to move!

Cindy and Ted watched through the car windows moving by as Sherlock swung forward on the luggage rack to where Cindy had been sitting. Soon, the train had gone far enough that they could no longer see the monkey. Ted held his breath and counted the seconds: Ten ... twelve, thirteen, fourteen. . . . They spotted Sherlock's brown fur at the door of the car. He swung out a little as if trying to find a way to get off the train unharmed. Nimbly, he climbed to the roof of the train, holding onto the book. Then he saw his chance as the train moved toward a signal pole.

Sherlock jumped from the train, grabbing the pole. He paused for a moment, then slid down the pole like a fireman on call.

Ted let out his breath. Sherlock loped back to the platform. Calmly, Sherlock handed Cindy the book, climbed back up onto her shoulder, and reached out to Ted for the popcorn. Cindy gave Sherlock a pat.

Ted was astonished by the little monkey's feat. "How'd you teach him to *do* that?" he asked.

"It was elementary," she said, making a face at her own joke. "Right, Sherlock?"

Maybe having Sherlock and Cindy here for two weeks would be pretty interesting after all, thought Ted, as the trio walked away from the station.

Long Ago in Finlay

A couple of days later, Ted and Cindy sat on a park bench near the fountain in the town square at the center of Finlay. Sherlock climbed all over them and the nearby statue of General Phineas Finlay while the cousins talked.

Ted was really getting to like Cindy. She'd lived in a lot of places and done a lot of unusual things, but she didn't brag about it. She was just interesting.

So was her monkey. Cindy had gotten him from her father, who was a zoologist. He studied animals all over the world.

"One day," Cindy explained to Ted, "Dad came across a female monkey who'd been killed by hunters. He was upset about that, but he was more upset by the fact that she had a newborn baby. The baby's arm was broken, too."

"Sherlock?"

"That's right. Dad brought Sherlock home and I helped take care of him. I fed him with a bottle. Even after his arm healed, we could never let him live in the wild again because he grew up in our house. Sherlock has never wanted to leave me, but Dad says he'll have to go to the zoo soon. Monkeys need special care and have to have monkey friends. As Dad says, 'People really don't make very good pets for monkeys.'"

Then Ted asked his cousin, "So you just came to Finlay because your dad was suddenly called away on one of his expeditions, and your mom wanted to go with him?"

"Sort of," Cindy replied, sensing some suspicion on the part of Ted. "I mean, I also thought it would be super to meet my long lost cousin, and —"

"Oh, you did?" said Ted, smiling. "But you're the one who's 'long lost.' I've lived here in Finlay all my life. So have Mom and her mom, and *her* mom — "

"I know, I know. All the way back to Great-Granny Morehouse. I was just being funny. Don't forget that Great-Granny Morehouse is my great-grandmother, too. She's the first one who owned the tektite locket — at least the first one in our family." Cindy snapped open the locket around her neck.

"Tektite? What's that?" Ted asked. The word gave him an odd feeling.

"That's the green stone on the outside." Cindy closed the locket. "At least, I think it's tektite. I wish I could find out for sure — it could be a piece of a meteorite!" Cindy finished excitedly.

Ted hesitated and then decided to satisfy his curiosity. He asked, "Could I examine the locket, Cindy?" She reached behind her neck with both hands, opened the clasp, carefully removed the locket, and handed it to Ted.

Also with care, Ted pushed the catch on the

egg-sized locket, and the green stone on the hinged cover swung away to reveal the picture inside of Great-Granny Morehouse — a very close resemblance to Cindy, as Ted's mother had said. In the picture, she was wearing the locket Ted now held. The green stone in the photograph seemed to sparkle as the real one did in his hand.

"What do you think the answer to the mystery is?" Ted asked.

"Well," Cindy said, "the only thing anyone alive seems to know about it is that Great-Granny Morehouse would never tell where she got it. That's a picture of her when she was about thirty years old. That's strange, considering she was my age when she got the locket, and she always *swore* the picture was already in it — " She stopped talking abruptly.

"Ted?" she asked, studying his reaction closely. "Why don't we find out where the locket came from?"

"Why?" Ted asked suspiciously. "You sound like you think she might have stolen it."

"I'd sure like to think she didn't, but maybe

she did. This green stone is pretty rare. I think maybe if it was stolen, old Finlay police records would show it."

"Swell idea," Ted said. "But forget it. Almost all of the town's historical records were destroyed by a fire a long time ago."

"So much for idea number one," Cindy replied, disappointed. Then, brightening, "But I'll bet there is a way to find out just where this locket came from. Want to try, long lost cousin?"

"Sure," Ted replied, "but how?"

At that moment, Sherlock appeared at her arm and started chattering at her persistently.

"Okay, boy," she said. "We'll find you some popcorn. Come on, Ted, Sherlock's hungry." Together, they walked across the town square toward a small building with a sign that read: KANDY KIOSK.

On their way Ted played tour guide.

"There's the new Finlay Exhibition Center." Ted pointed across Main Street to their right. "It just opened and Mom says they've got a neat exhibit called 'Long Ago in Finlay.' Want to check it out?"

"Sure!" Cindy said. "Maybe we'll find a clue about the locket." Ted glared at her. Why hadn't *he* thought of that? They crossed the street to the building. Sherlock's popcorn would have to wait.

As they came up to the door, they both stopped to stare. The announcement board for Today's Events listed KOHOUTEK THE GREAT, and pictured a magician. He was giving a free magic show in fifteen minutes. What stopped them, though, was his photo. It was the man with the piercing eyes and the small, square mustache.

"I saw that guy getting off of the train you came here on!" Ted said.

"I sat next to him on the train," said Cindy. "We talked a bit. He even asked to see my locket. He never told me he was a magician. It figures, though, considering the way he was dressed."

"Weird," said Ted. "Come on, let's go on in." Cindy tucked Sherlock into her backpack, just in case there was a rule against monkeys.

Together, they entered and followed signs to "Long Ago in Finlay." The exhibit focused on the town fire in 1930, a fire of unknown origin. A series of old photographs showed some of the extensive damage done. The charred remains of several buildings in the center of town stood blackly against a white winter background. Finlay had to be practically rebuilt afterward. Another series of pictures showed different things that had been located exactly where the Exhibition Center now stood. Few of these pictures were from before the great fire; most were from after.

"Look at this," said Cindy, pointing to a 1910 picture of a Victorian mansion with people walking in front of it. "I bet Great-Granny Morehouse saw that when she was a girl. Maybe she's even in this picture, but we don't recognize her."

"Sure, she saw that big house. She was born in 1900. Maybe that's her." He pointed to a young girl carrying a hand-basket.

"Wouldn't that be neat? Too bad the picture's too fuzzy to tell."

They looked at the rest of the Exhibition site

pictures. The mansion of 1910 had become the Finlay Museum by 1929. After it burned down in the fire "of mysterious origin" in 1930, the location had been used for temporary things — a circus in 1965, the 1976 bicentennial celebration, and even as the outdoor lot for a movie company in the 1950's.

"Well, this stuff doesn't tell us anything about the locket," Ted remarked disgustedly.

He was very wrong.

A Touch of Magic

"Look," said Ted. "There's the door of the auditorium where the magic show is going on. Want to go in?"

"Sure," answered Cindy. Quietly, so as not to disturb the audience, they opened the door and walked into the auditorium. They stood at the rear of the room. Kohoutek was on stage, speaking.

". . . two volunteers for my disappearing act." He put his hand on his forehead as if he were concentrating. "Ah! There they are. You, standing in the back of the auditorium. Yes, you two! Come on down to the stage."

Ted looked at Cindy uneasily.

Cindy nudged her cousin. "Come on!" she urged.

Why not? thought Ted. But why had the magician picked them? Then Ted remembered that Kohoutek had sat with Cindy and Sherlock on the train. Ted shrugged and followed Cindy to the stage.

After all, he thought, nobody ever *really* disappears in the middle of a magic trick.

"Here come my volunteers, folks," Kohoutek chattered to the audience. "Let's give them a hand. They don't know what they are about to get into!" The audience laughed; so did Cindy. Ted didn't think that was so funny.

Kohoutek went on: "Why, I remember the last time I was in Finlay — that was in 1976 at the bicentennial celebration — there was a young man who helped me. He had very long hair. Oh, that reminds me of a riddle I'd like to share with you. What is named for long hair but has no hair at all?" But Kohoutek didn't wait for an answer, for by then Ted and Cindy had reached the stage.

"Just come on up these stairs here," Kohoutek directed, "and tell us who you are." They introduced themselves.

The magician led them to the center of the stage. Behind them was a table with the props for Kohoutek's magic tricks. On the floor beside it stood a large antique mirror. Now what's that for? Ted wondered. No time to find out now, though; Kohoutek was starting the trick.

"Now, I want to show you something," the magician began. "Ted, you stay where you are. Cindy, you come over here. Oh, hello, Sherlock." Sherlock had just stuck his head up out of Cindy's backpack. The audience laughed. Sherlock loved it. He climbed onto Cindy's shoulder.

Kohoutek continued. "Now, Cindy, let me have that locket you are wearing."

"Sure," she agreed with a sly smile. "If you let me have your magic wand!" Everyone laughed.

"Now, there's nothing to fear. You can trust me. What I'm going to do to your locket, I did to the Hope Diamond."

Cindy turned to the audience.

"Quick, someone call the Smithsonian, please. Is the Hope Diamond still there?" The audience laughed.

Way to go, Cindy, thought Ted admiringly. She really knew how to handle this guy.

When people stopped laughing, Cindy agreeably reached behind her neck with both hands for the clasp of the locket. The locket was gone from her neck! She paled.

"Oh, Cindy," said Kohoutek smoothly. "Is *this* what you're looking for?" He dangled the locket from his hand and Cindy gasped with relief. Everyone laughed again — this time because Cindy had been fooled by Kohoutek.

Ted realized that the magician must have removed the locket from Cindy's neck as he had led them to center stage. But how? Ted decided to watch more carefully. He knew, because he had read some books about magic, that a magician always tries to make you look one place while the "magic" takes place in another.

Kohoutek held the locket in his right hand. He put it, and the chain, into his closed right fist and began to mumble some "magic" words, weird-sounding stuff— "*I Gameh T Fono Itaroda S'ot-toig.*" He held his right fist to his mouth and began to blow into it as if inflating a balloon.

No, Ted thought. Don't look at his right hand, look at his *left* hand, which is behind his back. From where he stood, Ted could just see the glint of the gold chain. Ah ha! He knew what the trick was. He figured nobody in the audience could see what he could from the stage near Kohoutek. He watched, fascinated, and when Kohoutek opened his empty right hand, everybody clapped. Ted, however, kept his eyes glued to the magician's left hand. And a good thing, too, for much to Ted's horror, he watched Kohoutek throw the locket behind him. Not just behind him, he threw it at the mirror.

Ted lunged to try to catch the locket before it crashed into the glass, but he was too late. The locket disappeared noiselessly right into the mirror! Ted braced himself for a crash but, oddly, found the glass presented no resistance. He, too, disappeared into the mirror.

24

Sherlock had been watching these strange events and began chattering excitedly to Cindy.

But Cindy ignored him and the cheering audience. Her eyes were fixed on Kohoutek to see what happened to her locket. Sherlock leaped into the arms of the magician, and then immediately jumped back down to the stage.

Sherlock had taken Kohoutek's pocket watch! The monkey held it out toward the audience, who laughed and clapped. Kohoutek was so startled he couldn't speak.

Imitating the master magician, and after chattering in monkeyese, Sherlock held his right hand to his mouth and mimed blowing into it, as if inflating a balloon. With his left hand, to which he had quickly transferred the watch, he flipped Kohoutek's watch into the mirror. Then he dove in after it.

Cindy paused only a moment to glare at Kohoutek, and then followed Sherlock into the mirror, leaving Kohoutek alone on the stage before a cheering audience.

The search had begun.

Spirit of '76

There was a long, loud whistling sound overhead and then a thunderous explosion.

Ka — BOOM. It was followed by a flurry of lesser explosions. Pop! Pop! *POP!*

Ted looked up, turning to the sound of the tremendous noise in the sky, but he was thunderstruck inside, too. What on earth had happened?

The night lit up with a strange twilight glow as a giant orange flower burst from the center of the explosion. First Ted, then Sherlock, and finally Cindy, appeared in the middle of a very big crowd.

As the orange flower faded and disappeared, everyone around them seemed to sigh at once. "Aaaahhhhhhh!"

Fireworks.

They had landed, if that was the right word, in the middle of a Fourth of July celebration!

Ted was mystified by the sudden transport from the theater stage. It hadn't been the Fourth of July when they'd walked into the magic show — it hadn't even been nighttime. And they'd gone from inside to outdoors — *through* a mirror!

Besides those few minor things, Ted groaned inwardly, everything seemed to be just fine.

"Cindy," Ted whispered, "Kohoutek threw your locket through the mirror. I saw it happen! And then I followed it!"

"Yeah, then Sherlock threw Kohoutek's watch after it," she told Ted. "And then *we* followed you."

Ted thought Cindy was being strangely matter-of-fact about these incredible events. In fact, she dropped to her hands and knees and began searching around on the ground. Sherlock imitated her, except that he kept one hand on his ear. When the next overhead explosion and flash of light came, Sherlock covered his other ear, screeched, and jumped up and down in protest. Sherlock clearly didn't like fireworks. Meanwhile, Cindy scrambled around looking for the locket in the temporary light.

Some of the people nearby were finding the silly girl and the nutty monkey more interesting than the fireworks. Ted noticed a very large policeman eyeing the three of them suspiciously. Cindy had found Kohoutek's watch, which was set in a jet-black stone. She looked puzzled as she stared at the watch in the red glare of another rocket.

"Cindy," Ted hissed. "Cindy, I think we'd better go." He nodded his head in the direction of the policeman.

But she seemed oblivious. " 'Named for the Captain of the Paramour,' this watch is inscribed. I wonder what on earth that means? Sounds like a play by Gilbert and Sullivan," she muttered.

Ted ignored her. "Let's get out of here," he

said, pulling on his cousin's arm. The policeman was now making his way toward them. Finally Cindy seemed to get the message and turned to look in the direction of the policeman, too.

Perhaps that was why the cousins didn't notice a dark-cloaked figure pick up the tektite locket from the ground, then disappear into the crowd.

Right then Sherlock sniffed the wind and ran off. The cousins plunged through the crowd after him.

They caught up with Sherlock at the Kandy Kiosk across the town square. Ted asked the saleswoman for Sherlock's popcorn, because Cindy's mind was on something else. Cindy was staring up at a huge banner strung across two poles:

–1776 —— FINLAY BICENTENNIAL CELEBRATION —— 1976–

"Ted," she gasped, a little out of breath from chasing Sherlock, and, perhaps, a little frightened, "I think something very strange has happened."

Ted had to agree. "Something *very* strange."

He was so shaken that he gave the woman one of his special dollar coins for Sherlock's popcorn and waited for change. His heart was beating very fast as he tried to consider everything at once. He realized suddenly that the popcorn lady was eyeing him suspiciously.

"Look here, son," she said, glaring at the coin. "If this is supposed to be some kinda joke, fine. But how about paying me with real money?" She handed back Ted's Susan B. Anthony dollar.

"What do you mean?" Ted asked her.

"Maybe the woman on this coin is important," she said, pointing at the money with her index finger. "But I also know she ain't on a real coin. What is it, some kind of historical souvenir? So how about fifty cents worth of real money? Or am I supposed to get it from your monkey?"

Ted fished two quarters from his pocket. The popcorn lady looked at the quarters closely, tapped them on the glass of the popcorn machine to make sure they "rang true," and then tossed them into her cash drawer.

Cindy had sat on a nearby park bench and

Sherlock scampered over to perch on the back. Ted walked over and joined them.

"I heard," Cindy said.

"What on earth do we do now?" Ted asked.

"It's 1976, right? But we're still in Finlay and we're still at the place where the Exhibition Center belongs, right?"

"Right," Ted answered. "That's the same candy stand as the one in the time we came from."

"Then we've gone back in time to a previous 'existence' of the building. In fact, we saw a picture of it at the exhibit, right?"

"Yes, I follow you," Ted agreed.

"Then," she said, standing up, "obviously what we've got to do is to find Kohoutek."

"Kohoutek!" Ted exclaimed. "Now I *don't* follow. What you do mean, obviously? He's back *there.*" Ted was getting upset, and was almost shouting.

Cindy replied, "Keep your voice down " — she nodded toward the popcorn stand where the popcorn lady was speaking to the tall policeman and pointing in their direction — "if you're going to pass phony money." She even managed to smile.

Ted didn't find this funny at all.

They started walking rapidly away, with Sherlock bringing up the rear and pausing to eat some of his popcorn.

Cindy said, "I don't really know what Kohoutek has to do with all this. That's exactly what we have to find out. But I want my locket back and I have a strong hunch that if we find Kohoutek we find the locket. But to do that, we'll have to be pretty good searchers."

"Okay, then that's what we are: the searchers. Come on, fellow-searcher. Kohoutek must be at the bottom of this, right? We know he's here because while we walked up to the stage I heard him mention that the last time he was in Finlay, he came to the bicentennial celebration."

"That's it!" Cindy said. "Right now, though, I think we'd better split up. I have a feeling all of this would be a little hard to explain to that policeman." She half turned around, just enough to see that he was still following them. "Can you handle him?" she asked Ted. "I'll see if I can find out where Kohoutek is. Meet me in front of the Kandy Kiosk in a half hour and we'll figure out what to do then. See you later!" With that, Cindy dashed off. Sherlock handed Ted the popcorn box and sprinted after her. Ted turned in time to hear the tall policeman, a few steps away, say,

"Just a minute, son. I want to talk to you."

A Happy Medium

Cindy stood hesitantly at the doorway of a shop on Main Street. Sherlock peeked over her shoulder from the backpack.

The sign outside read:

MADAME JUDITH BIELA

YOUR FORTUNE TOLD

WHILE — U — WAIT

Inside, the shop was lit by dozens of candles burning in little plates.

"I've been expecting you," said an old woman,

turning her chair so she could face Cindy.

"How could you have been expecting me?" Cindy asked as she walked toward the table where Madame Biela sat. "I only decided to come in a moment ago, and then only to ask directions. And how could you tell someone's fortune if she *didn't* wait? I mean, the way your sign says."

"Cross my palm with paper," said Madame Biela, "and I'll tell you."

"Paper?" Cindy asked incredulously. "Not silver?"

"Yeah, word's out around town that some kids have been using phony coins, so everyone's being very careful about money."

"How'd you hear that?" Cindy asked.

"The spirit of Alexander, he spoke to me —"

"Alexander?"

"Yeah, Alexander Graham Bell. You know what I mean. Someone called me on the phone!"

"Listen." Cindy picked up a candle from a chair at the table and sat down, while Sherlock perched on her shoulder. "What I'd like to know is how to find a man named Kohoutek. I have to return his watch."

"You have the jet-stone watch?" Madame Biela asked. Cindy nodded.

"Donati Kohoutek?" the old woman continued.

"I don't know," Cindy said. "But there can't be too many people named Kohoutek with a watch like this. Suppose you tell me where this Donati is."

"I never heard of him," said the fortune teller. She unveiled a crystal in the center of the table. *"Remonortsa Layor D Noces,"* she chanted. "It's cloudy, very cloudy. I suspect from the crystal that the source of what you seek is Oort's Cloud."

"What makes you think I'm seeking anything besides Kohoutek? And he's not from Oort, but from Chillicothe, Ohio — he told me so on the train. Anyway, *I* don't see any cloud," Cindy said, peering at the globe on the table.

"You sure as shootin' shouldn't. That thing's bonafide Czech crystal. Look, kid, Kohoutek's show is in the old Day School auditorium down the block. That'll be two bucks."

"Two dollars!" Cindy said. "For what?"

"That's twenty-five cents for speaking the answer, and a dollar seventy-five for knowing the answer to speak."

Reluctantly, Cindy gave Madame Biela two dollar bills. "Shouldn't I get a fortune for this, too?"

"Certainly." Madame Biela picked up a large card from the top of the Tarot deck on the table. It was The Tower.

The old woman gasped. "Beware of change by water, my child," she chanted. "Beware of change by water."

A breeze blew through the open door and all of Madame Biela's candles flickered and went out. Cindy, with Sherlock now nestled in the backpack, turned and walked out onto the sidewalk.

She walked in the opposite direction from which she'd come, toward the "old Day School

auditorium." There, according to Madame Biela, she would find Kohoutek and, Cindy hoped, the locket.

In the front of the building was a sign announcing Kohoutek's magic show. Cindy peered into the darkened, filled auditorium and there, on stage, was the magician being assisted by a long-haired young man. Cindy slipped around to a backstage entrance and found Kohoutek's dressing room. She recognized it by the boxes and equipment she had seen on the train. She hesitated to look through the magician's belongings, but what choice did she have?

When she went over to the dressing table, she was surprised to find her locket among other jewelry on the table. Kohoutek *must* have picked it up at the fireworks exhibition. Relieved to have it back, she slipped it around her neck and left the watch in place of the locket on the dressing table. She turned to leave through the door but, hearing the loud applause of the audience on the other side of the wall, went instead to the window and opened it. Sherlock jumped from her backpack onto the windowsill and out onto the ground.

Just then, Kohoutek came into the dressing room from the stage.

"Cindy!" he said, astonished to see her.

"I've switched them," she answered him as she sat on the windowsill. "You've got your watch. I've got my locket. Good-bye." She swung her legs through the open window and dropped to the ground.

"It's not *yours* now. Don't you see?" Kohoutek said to her, leaning out the window.

"It certainly *is*! Leave me alone!" she said, turning away.

"Cindy, give it to me. You don't understand. . . ." He began to climb out the window after her.

"I guess I *do* understand," she retorted, looking over her shoulder. She began running after Sherlock, toward her rendezvous with Ted. Kohoutek was only a few steps behind.

Still, she was a fast runner.

Change by Water

Ted knew he was in for it now. The policeman, Officer D'Arrest, his name badge said, was calling Ted's parents from a pay phone to verify Ted's story. Ted was beginning to wonder if always telling the truth was such a good idea. He wondered, too, if the policeman's name was a bad sign of things to come.

"So you *do* have a son named Ted," D'Arrest was saying into the phone, all the while glaring at Ted. "But he's a toddler and home in bed? Thank you very much, ma'am," the policeman said. He hung up and turned toward Ted.

Ted ran.

He ran across the Town Square, past the statue of General Finlay, and toward the Kandy Kiosk where he had agreed to meet Cindy. D'Arrest, blowing his whistle, followed, but was having a hard time keeping up. Suddenly, Ted saw Cindy and Sherlock running toward the Kiosk from another direction. Kohoutek, red-and-black cape flapping, was chasing *her*. Ted heard him shout,

"Cindy, wait. Please wait! You don't understand. . . ."

"C'mon, Ted," she shouted, and looked both ways before darting across the street to the field where the fireworks display had been.

Between puffs, as they ran, she explained to Ted, "I found my locket among the costume jewelry in Kohoutek's dressing room. I exchanged my locket for his watch. By then his show was over and he saw me as I was leaving. What happened to you?"

"I told the policeman what my name was, like he asked. He called my folks. I'm supposed to be a little kid home in bed."

"Oh, boy, we'd *better* get out of here," Cindy said.

They had reached the base of a tower in the field and Sherlock scrambled up it.

"No, Sherlock. That's no way out!" shouted Cindy. When Sherlock didn't stop, she chased up after him. Ted paused until he saw that Kohoutek and D'Arrest had nearly reached the base of the tower. There was nowhere else to go. He scrambled up the tower after Cindy.

Sherlock was perched on a tiny platform when Ted and Cindy reached him. They looked down and saw a very large tub of water below. The starry night was reflected on the surface.

"Oh, no," said Ted. "This contraption is part of an act where a lunatic named Tuttle skydives twenty-five feet into a shallow tub of water. He does it every July Fourth."

"Swell," Cindy snapped. "Let's come back next year and find out what to do next!"

Kohoutek was climbing up the tower and it was swaying dizzyingly, obviously not having been built for two kids, a monkey, and a magician.

"Cindy, Ted, wait. . . ." Kohoutek was shouting as Sherlock lost his grip and fell from the tower and Cindy lunged after him. Ted felt his own grip loosen and he, too, tumbled toward the water.

Ted saw Sherlock and Cindy splash down just before he hit the water himself. He thought their landing had been surprisingly soft, considering how high up the tower they had been.

Then they seemed to sink for a very long time. Funny thing, thought Ted. Tuttle's Tank is only three feet deep.

Still they sank.

Museum Quality

The next thing Ted noticed was that he was cold. Not wet, but cold. Beside him Cindy and Sherlock huddled together. All three of them were sitting on a park bench. Wherever or whenever they had landed, it wasn't the evening of July 4th, 1976, anymore. It was daytime, and there was snow on the ground!

"When have we gotten ourselves into now?" Ted asked.

"I don't know, but if we don't get ourselves inside someplace, we'll all get pneumonia."

Ted looked around to get his bearings. They

were still in Finlay, all right. But it wasn't anything like their own time — or even 1976. There was the Kandy Kiosk. But it was a plain newsstand. The cars on the street were antiques! A Victorian mansion stood where the Exhibition Center should have been.

"Look, the old mansion. That was standing until 1930, and judging by the look of these cars, that's about where we are now. You know, we seem to be visiting the exact times we saw in the Exhibition Center pictures. So what do we do now?" he asked his cousin.

"I haven't been working on *what*. I've been working on *why*. *Why* does Kohoutek want this locket so badly? Do you think it's fantastically valuable or something?"

"If only we could take it to a jewelry store or...."

"... or a museum."

'That's it!" said Ted. "The old mansion. It was a museum in 1930. Let's go!"

Together, they hurried across the street to the old house. The sign on the lawn read:

FINLAY MUSEUM AND HISTORICAL SOCIETY
G. HARRINGTON ABELL, CURATOR.

Ted opened the door and a bell tinkled. Inside, they were greeted by a welcoming fire crackling in the fireplace. They stood by it, warming themselves, until a white-haired man with a cane came into the room and introduced himself as Mr. Abell.

The cousins told him their names and Cindy explained, "We're here to see if you could tell us something about this locket."

Cindy handed it to him.

"Very interesting," he said. A jeweler's glass seemed to appear in his hand. "Very interesting."

"Is it valuable?"

"Well, that depends," Mr. Abell said. "This green stone could be a tektite." Cindy grinned. "I'd like to verify that with some instruments in my lab. Would you wait here, please?"

"You won't damage the locket, will you?"

"No, you can trust me. I won't do anything to the locket that I didn't also do to the Hope

Diamond," he said, walking to the back hallway that led to the stairs.

Ted and Cindy were only too happy to stay by the fire. Sherlock, whose natural habitat was a tropical forest, seemed very relieved to be warm again.

Just as they began to feel thawed, the big front door opened, letting in a rush of cold air. The fire roared and crackled in response to the draft.

"Hi!" a man called to them from the door. "Sorry to keep you waiting. I don't usually get many visitors at this time of day. I'll be right with you."

"Who are you?" Cindy asked.

"I'm Harry Abell, the cura—"

He didn't have time to finish the word. Cindy and Ted exchanged looks and sprinted for the back hallway where the white-haired man had gone with Cindy's locket. Sherlock clung to Cindy's shoulder. They took the stairs as fast as they could.

But they were too late.

What they found was an empty room on the second floor. There was an open window. A ladder reached from the window to the ground. On a chair by the window were all the clothes the phony Mr. Abell had been wearing. On a table, they found a white-haired wig, a latex mask, a cane, and an instant camera.

"Cindy," said Ted. "That wasn't G. Harrington Abell, Curator. That was — "

" — Kohoutek. I know. I just remembered he said the same thing about the Hope Diamond at the magic show." She looked at the camera for a moment. "I wonder who he took a picture of," she mused.

On the windowsill lay a Tarot card. On one side was The Magician. On the other, the card read:

DONATI KOHOUTEK
Master Magician
1066 Hastings
Bayeux
(141) 989-1986

Trial by Fire

"What's going on here?" Mr. Abell demanded breathlessly as he entered the room.

"There was another man here. He said he was you. He took — "

"Nonsense!" the old man declared. "You kids are just trying to fiddle faddle me. I won't have it! Now get out of here — you and that filthy creature! Out! You don't belong in a museum!"

Cindy and Ted exchanged glances. It seemed that no matter what decade they were in, grown-ups got angry with them. Still, there was no point in arguing with the real Mr. Abell. Resigned, Cindy tucked Sherlock into her backpack and they followed Mr. Abell down the stairs.

They felt a chilly blast of air. Mr. Abell must have left the door open in his rush to follow them upstairs. They realized they could hear crackling fire, too, and smell smoke. Mr. Abell reached the main room first.

"Oh no!" he cried. "The fire! It's caught onto the curtains!"

The cousins could see the blaze licking at the tall curtains as they came to the bottom of the stairs. Somehow, when the fire caught the draft, it must have flared or shot out a hot coal that started the curtains on fire. Quickly, the blaze jumped from one curtain to the next. Mr. Abell pulled off his coat and began trying to beat the fire out.

"Help me!" he begged. He didn't have to ask twice. The cousins came to his aid. Cindy tried to stamp out a fresh fire that had started on the carpet while Ted brought a step stool so Mr. Abell could reach the top flames.

"It's no use," the old man said. "I'm going to get the Fire Department. You kids get out of here!" Mr. Abell ran out the door yelling, "Fire! Fire!" as he headed for the fire station on the other side of the town green.

The flames grew bigger and hotter by the second. Cindy and Ted couldn't believe how quickly the fire had spread in the old wooden building.

"Let's go!" said Cindy.

"Wait a sec," Ted said. "Wouldn't there be a fire hose next to the stairs in a public building?"

"Right! Let's see if we can help before the firemen come."

Together, they ran back toward the stairs. There *was* a fire closet, with a glass door and a fire hose inside. As they got closer to it, they saw that it seemed to glow. It wasn't the hose glowing, though. The flames right behind them were reflected in the glass door.

"Cindy! Let's go for it!" said Ted, running to break the glass and grab the hose.

"I'm right here," she cried, holding onto him.

The cousins lunged for the glass door and went through it. The last thing they saw before leaving 1930 was an orange wall of fire right behind them.

Edmund and Isaac

"Where's the hose?" demanded Ted.

"I don't think we need it now," Cindy answered as she felt around. She, Ted, and Sherlock were all crammed into some kind of box. Cindy reached upward. The lid budged. "We seem to be packed into a trunk. I hear voices outside. Let's see what's going on."

Ted lifted the lid an inch and the cousins peered out at two men in knee breeches and white periwigs who were arguing nearby. Cindy tried to soothe Sherlock, who squirmed in her arms. She studied the scene, too. The cousins

wanted to figure out where they were now *before* emerging. Ted let the trunk close slowly. "Well?" he asked. "Where are we?"

"Definitely Cambridge University in England," Cindy whispered to Ted. "I recognize the sandstone buildings and the spire of St. Mary the Great. That's the good news. The bad news is that I'm afraid something has *really* slipped this time. Those men are dressed the way people dressed three hundred years ago!"

"Yeah, I see," said Ted. "One of them is even dressed like George Washington!"

He lifted the lid again and they listened to the men talking.

"Isaac Newton," said the one pacing in front of the other man, "I don't agree with you about your manuscript. It's the most important book about science ever written."

"I appreciate your compliment, Edmund," said Isaac. "But the simple truth is that no one wants to publish it. Therefore, it cannot be very important," he concluded as he reached for an apple from the bowl on the table.

Ted poked Cindy in the ribs. "Cindy!" he exclaimed under his breath. "That's Isaac Newton, the one with the apple. He was the most important scientist in the world before Einstein. He even invented gravity."

Cindy gave him a withering look. "And Fig Newtons? Don't you mean he *discovered* gravity?"

"Yeah, I guess."

They turned their attention to the other man, who spoke again.

"Well, if they won't publish it, then by the four Moons of Jupiter, I'll publish it myself, if you'll let me...."

Suddenly, Sherlock squirmed free of Cindy's arms, squeezed through the open trunk lid, and made a beeline toward a startled Newton. Sherlock grabbed for the apple.

An angry bellow came from behind them: "Cut! Cut! *CUT!*"

The man who had bellowed threw open the lid of the trunk. Ted and Cindy emerged sheepishly to face a very angry person wearing sunglasses and a gold neck scarf. Behind him were three very large cameras and many bright lights. The man was a movie director!

"Who let those kids and that monkey on the set?" the director raged. "We're going to have to shoot the whole scene over again. Get them *off* the property!"

And with that, Ted and Cindy, with Sherlock in tow, were escorted out by a security guard. They left through a gate in the tall wooden fence that surrounded what they now knew was the outdoor lot for a movie studio on the Exhibition Center site. They had seen a photograph of it — taken in 1956.

"See ya later, alligator," the guard said, smugly, as he slammed the gate behind them.

"Sure. After 'while, crocodile," Ted replied in disgust.

Saved by the Gong

It was a beautiful autumn afternoon in Finlay. Gold and red leaves covered the trees and the ground around them. But Ted and Cindy were much too upset to notice. Things seemed to go from bad to worse for them.

"Bad enough Kohoutek got my locket," Cindy said. "But it was really a shame we couldn't stop the fire," she added as they walked away from the movie studio.

"It's a shame we can't save ourselves from bouncing around in Finlay's history," Ted replied, annoyed. "Anyway," he continued, "I don't think we *can* change anything in the past. And even if we could change things, I don't think it would be such a good idea."

"I suppose you're right," said Cindy. "After all, when we tried to put out the fire, we already knew the great fire had destroyed the museum and some of the town, too. At least we learned how it started. The fire's 'mysterious origin' was a blast of cold air."

"Cindy, how do you think we'll ever get back to our own time? I'll bet my mom is getting pretty worried about us."

"I was wondering about that, too," Cindy said. "And Sherlock's try for Newton's apple doesn't mean he's the only one who's hungry. I sure could do with something to eat."

"How can we pay for food, Cindy?" Ted asked. "We don't have enough money."

As if in answer, a deep, booming noise rang across the town square. Ted and Cindy looked across the street to see the sun glinting off a huge brass Chinese gong suspended from an intricately carved arch. It stood in front of the building where Cindy had spoken with Madame Biela. A smiling proprietor held the large mallet. Madame Biela's mysterious sign was no longer evident. Now, a sign in the window proclaimed:

GRAND OPENING

TEMPLE ONE CHINESE RESTAURANT

HAVE YOUR FIRST MEAL HERE ON THE HOUSE

W E L C O M E

As they crossed the street, Cindy said, "Looks like we can stop worrying about having our next meal, Ted. Boy, if you want attention for your new restaurant, a giant gong seems a great way to get it!"

When they were seated, the proprietor came to their table. "For you, I will bring *Grotto Shinas*," he said. Within minutes, the cousins were served a delicious lunch. They followed their meal with fortune cookies and tea. Much as they enjoyed the food, the only thing on their minds while they ate was how they could get home.

"Here," Ted said, handing Cindy her fortune cookie. "Maybe that'll tell us what to do next. Mine just said I would go on a long voyage. Was that ever right! I just wish we could shorten up this voyage, don't you, Cindy?"

Cindy didn't seem to hear him as she read from a small pink slip of paper her "fortune" from the cookie. "Ted," she said excitedly, handing him the fortune. "I think I know how to get home. Or at least how to leave 1956."

With that, she got up and walked out of the restaurant with Sherlock on her shoulder. Ted read the fortune: TO GET WHERE YOU'RE GOING, RE-FLECT ON WHERE YOU'VE BEEN.

After thanking the proprietor, he trailed Cindy out of the restaurant in puzzlement.

When he got to the door, Cindy and Sherlock were staring into the gong. He stood next to them, wondering what they would do next.

"Don't you see, Ted?" Cindy asked.

Ted looked at Cindy's reflection in the shiny surface of the gong. Suddenly he understood what Cindy had figured out — how they were traveling through time. Together they stepped forward toward their reflections. They felt as if they were being pulled right through the gong. Once again, they were headed for another time.

Knockdown

Cindy gave Ted's arm a hard tug, yanking him onto the curb where she stood. This saved Ted from being run down by a speeding wagon pulled by a team of horses. It had a load of ice blocks, and a sign that read: BROOKS ICE HOUSE.

Horses and wagons? Ice? thought Ted. Where had they got to now? Or more appropriately, *when?*

The wagon stopped. The teamster casually removed his foot from the dashboard, pushed the brake forward, and slowly turned back to Ted and Cindy.

"Son, if you want to live to see these here ice blocks turned into works of art by the local Michelangelos, you'll watch how many wagons you step in front of. Y'hear?"

Without waiting to see Ted's eager nod, he turned, released the brake, flicked the reins, and drove off toward the Finlay town square.

"Thanks, Cindy," said Ted, somewhat sheepishly.

Cindy nodded. "Don't mention it. Looks like we've gone even further back this time. What do you think?" They started toward the town square, Sherlock holding Cindy's hand.

"It sure feels like long ago," Ted said, glancing around. "What cars there are seem to be the old-fashioned kind — 'horseless carriages,' weren't they called?"

"Yup. Definitely 1910. Should we find out who lives in the old mansion across the town green?" Cindy asked, pointing at the old — or maybe new — building.

Suddenly Ted pulled her and Sherlock behind a tree and put his index finger to his lips. A familiar, mustached man in evening clothes and a top hat was walking diagonally across the town square. He frequently referred to a pocket watch set in a jet-black stone. His concern about the time was probably why he didn't notice the two cousins.

It was Kohoutek.

"I wonder if he's getting around the same way we are," whispered Cindy.

"I don't know," Ted answered. "But it seems as if every time we do something to get the locket back, he's right there to mess it up. He seems to know something we don't. Maybe this time we can learn something if *we* follow *him*."

They eased back onto the path from behind the tree, and trailed Kohoutek at what they thought was a safe distance.

"Look, Ted, the locket!" Cindy said excitedly, pointing at Kohoutek. He had taken the tektite locket out of his hat and held it in his hand. Kohoutek was standing on the corner and glancing down the block as if waiting to meet someone.

"That's a very interesting monkey you've got

there, youngsters," a voice from behind them said. They turned to see a policeman. He stood a couple of paces away. "And suppose you tell me why you're following that gentleman, Mr. Kohoutek, on this May morning."

"You know him?" Ted asked.

"Never mind what I know. Mr. Kohoutek told me at supper last night at the boardinghouse that he was being annoyed by some youngsters and asked me to keep an eye out for you."

"Kohoutek has stolen my tektite locket," Cindy said. "And — "

"Well now, suppose we just go ask Mr. Kohoutek about your accusation and then maybe discuss it with your folks. You do have folks, do you not?"

As they approached Kohoutek, Ted and Cindy could see a girl in a bonnet, wearing a pinafore and carrying a basket. She was walking toward where Kohoutek stood. Suddenly, Kohoutek looked up and saw the policeman and the cousins.

He sprinted off in the opposite direction. Looking back over his shoulder, he bowled over the young girl in the bonnet. He paused to pick up her hand-basket and return it to her, then continued to run off.

"Maybe you kids are right about this citizen," the policeman shouted, as he chased after the magician who was so good at disappearing.

Thin Ice

"Are you all right?" Cindy asked, offering her hand to the girl Kohoutek had knocked down.

"I don't know," said the girl. "Last night I thought I saw a shooting star. I'm certainly seeing stars now. A moment ago, I thought I saw a monkey on your shoulder. And looking at you, I feel like I'm looking at a picture of myself. I must be ill."

"You two *do* look alike," Ted said reflectively.

"And you *did* see a monkey. This is Sherlock," Cindy said, pulling Sherlock by the hand in front of her. "And this is my cousin, Ted Bennett." Ted nodded a hello. "And I'm Cindy Forbes."

"Thank you for your help. My name is Gwenith Encke," the girl began.

"Not Morehouse?" Ted asked, trying to hide his disappointment. Gwenith's appearance had made him think that maybe. . . .

"No, but if you are looking for the Morehouses', their son is in my class at the Finlay Day School. I don't know where he lives, but the school is over there." Gwenith pointed to the building where Kohoutek performed his magic show in 1976. "Now I'm going to see the ice sculptures on the town square, if you don't mind. Mr. Brooks is having the ice sculptures made to show that he has so much ice for iceboxes this summer that he can afford to melt some now. Isn't that fun?" Gwenith said. Then she added, "And thank you for your help."

As Gwenith walked off, Ted and Cindy saw the policeman approaching. He was holding Kohoutek firmly by the elbow.

"Now, suppose you people tell me what this is about before I run you all into the stationhouse."

"This man stole my tektite locket, Officer," Cindy said heatedly.

"Well, what about it, Mr. Kohoutek? Why did you run off?"

"I have no locket," Kohoutek responded calmly, holding up his arms as if asking to be searched. The policeman, accepting the magician's offer, uncovered quite an assortment of things.

From Kohoutek's cape, the officer first pulled out six colored-silk handkerchiefs. Next, he found five decks of cards. One was all aces. There were a magic wand, four doves, three eggs (hard-boiled, they assumed), and a scrap of paper that read: THE HEAVENS THEMSELVES BLAZE FORTH THE DEATH OF PRINCES.

"Is that in code?" Cindy demanded.

"No, that's in *Julius Caesar*," the magician answered matter-of-factly.

The policeman continued his search of Kohoutek's cape. He found six silver coins, one small white rabbit, two pouches of "magic dust" (sparkles), and the watch they had seen Kohoutek consult earlier.

The policeman stared at the watch set in its shiny jet-black stone.

"What's this rock around the clock?" the policeman demanded.

"It's obsidian," Kohoutek answered.

There was no locket.

"I'm sorry for disturbing you, Mr. Kohoutek. You obviously had no opportunity to dispose of any locket if you ever did have it. But you should be a bit more careful about how you knock children down on the sidewalks."

"Oh, but I was, Officer," Kohoutek said, cryptically.

"And you youngsters must be a bit more careful about accusing people. In fact," he said as if coming to a decision, "I believe I'll escort you home. Where do you live?"

Ted told him his parents' address. The policeman seemed confused.

"Is there a house there?" he demanded. Ted nodded. "Well, come on, then," the policeman said, and started across the town square.

Suddenly, nimble-fingered Sherlock grabbed

Kohoutek's watch from the magician's hand, then ran away in the direction of the ice sculptures. Cindy and Ted chased after him. The monkey headed for the biggest, uncarved block. It was shiny, glistening in the warm May sun. Sherlock disappeared into it.

Just before Ted and Cindy followed Sherlock, they heard a startled cry nearby. They looked over to see Gwenith Encke, whose hand-basket lay on the ground. Gwenith glanced wide-eyed from them to the open tektite locket that she held in her hand.

The policeman and Kohoutek rushed toward Ted and Cindy. But the cousins eluded them, stepping into their reflection in the shiny ice.

Picture Perfect

"That's impossible," Ted exclaimed, glancing at the circus Big Top that dominated the Finlay skyline that day. "That *can't* be where the locket came from."

Cindy sat on the park bench near Gale's Sweet Shoppe — the future Kandy Kiosk — and regarded Ted calmly. Sherlock twirled Kohoutek's watch and blew into his right hand experimentally.

"Look, I know it sounds weird, but our great-grandmother got the tektite locket from Kohoutek. He must have slipped it into her basket after he 'accidentally' bumped into her when the policeman chased him."

"Are you sure that was our great-grandmother? Her name wasn't right. I asked her because I thought she might have been Great-Granny Morehouse. She said it was Encke, not Morehouse."

"Of course, silly," Cindy said. "Encke was her *maiden* name. She became Morehouse when she married her classmate from the Finlay Day School — our great-grandfather. That had to be a long time after we met her."

"But then why wouldn't she ever say where the locket came from?" Ted asked.

"Would you?"

"No. I guess I wouldn't. She must have been dumbfounded by what happened to her that morning."

"You mean just because she saw a couple of strangers with a monkey being chased by a policeman and a magician disappear through a block of ice in the town square?" Cindy asked, smiling.

"No," Ted said seriously. "After all, the policeman also saw us. Too bad the town records got burned up in the museum fire. It would have been a lot of fun to read his report!" They laughed at the thought.

"Then why do you think she was amazed enough to keep the source of the locket a secret her whole life? I mean, she only died a few years ago." Ted watched as Sherlock hopped from Cindy's shoulder to his.

"Ah! It's elementary, my dear Sherlock, isn't it?" Ted asked mysteriously. Sherlock chattered in response.

"Not to me, it isn't. Tell me, Ted," Cindy said impatiently.

"Okay," Ted relented. "It was because the locket already had her picture in it."

"So what? That's hardly amazing. They had photography. Even in 1910. That's no big deal. Anyone could have taken her picture and put it in the locket."

"Not in Great-Granny's time! In those days, you had to sit still for a long time to have a picture taken. No one could take a picture of you without your knowing about it. And don't forget," Ted said triumphantly, "the picture in the locket when she got it was actually a picture of her when she was thirty years old. Don't you think it would be shocking to see a picture of how you'd look in the future?"

"It sure would. Hey!" Cindy said. "She was probably around thirty when the museum burned down. Remember the instant camera we found there with Kohoutek's card? I wonder. . . ."

"You mean you think he took the locket picture in 1930?" Ted asked.

"Yes," Cindy said. "And then he slipped the locket with his 1930 picture in it into her handbasket when he 'accidentally' bumped into her in 1910!"

"Weird!" said Ted.

"If we're so smart, fellow-searcher," Cindy went on, "we should be able to figure out where the locket came from in the first place. I mean, where was it before Great-Granny Morehouse got it from Kohoutek in 1910?"

"I know this sounds strange, Cindy, but where it was just before 1910 was in 1986. Somehow, time got all turned around and the locket went from Great-Granny Morehouse to you, through generations and then back again. In order for Great-Granny Morehouse to have it to leave to you, Kohoutek *had* to give it to her first. It went in a circle!"

"You mean the locket looped once in *time?*" Cindy said, amazed.

"Yeah," Ted answered. "And that means that the locket never existed before 1910 and stopped existing — except as history — after the moment Kohoutek threw it into the mirror."

Cindy shook her head in amazement. It sounded too strange, but it was the only explanation.

Sherlock continued twirling Kohoutek's timepiece on its chain as the cousins puzzled out the paradox of the tektite locket that was now gone forever. Ted took the watch from Sherlock and put it in his back pocket. Sherlock jumped up and down in protest.

"What about Kohoutek?" Cindy asked. "It doesn't look like he is such a bad guy after all, does it?"

"No. In fact, he's been trying to tell us something all along. Maybe he knew he *had* to get the locket back from our time to Great-Granny Morehouse, even if we tried to stop him. Another thing is possible, too. Maybe in order for things to work out right, we *had* to try to stop him."

"Right," Cindy said. "Because otherwise, if Kohoutek hadn't helped, and if we hadn't helped him, history wouldn't have turned out right. I wouldn't have had the locket to give back to Great-Granny, and she wouldn't have been able to hand it down to me in the first place if I hadn't...." She trailed off and shrugged to Ted. "It's still a bit confusing."

"You're right about that," Ted said. "Anyway, it's time to head back to our own time. Let's go, Sherlock."

"But how?" Cindy asked, catching up with them. "We seem to bounce around in time without ever knowing where we're going to wind up."

"The circus is in town, right?" Ted said, glancing at the Big Top on the horizon. "Well, this must be 1965. According to the pictures we saw, the circus in 1965 is the only Exhibition Center site activity we haven't already visited, right?"

"Right," Cindy agreed.

"And we got into all of this by walking through a *mirror*, not just a shiny reflecting thing like ice or glass or a gong, right? Well, let's go find another mirror."

They headed for the circus.

Familiar Ground

Ted and Cindy were simply not prepared for what happened next.

They followed hundreds of people who were streaming toward the circus. The first section they came to was the menagerie.

"Oh, good," Cindy said. "Sherlock loves me the most, but it's always good for him to visit with other monkeys. Otherwise, he gets lonely. Let's see if he has any cousins here."

They paused to buy some popcorn for Sherlock and then tucked him safely into the backpack once again.

A large crowd was milling around the menagerie. Ted's favorite part was the elephants. There even was a baby one.

Cindy was looking for monkeys. She cared about them and liked to see that they were well taken care of. Most performing animals are. People usually worried about monkeys who were kept as pets. With her father's advice, though, Cindy was always able to take good care of Sherlock.

A crowd was gathering near one cage.

"Come on, Ted," Cindy urged. "I think I hear monkeys over there." She pointed to her right. They both looked in that direction, but they didn't see a monkey cage. They found themselves looking straight at two redheaded teenage girls they recognized from pictures they had seen in their family albums.

"Mom!" Cindy blurted, staring at the tektite locket that one of the girls was wearing. "What are *you* doing here?"

The girl stared back at Cindy blankly. "Flake off, kid," she said. Ted thought the girls were teasing them.

"Listen, Mom," Ted began, speaking to the second girl. "I can explain everything. We were just going to the Exhibition Center and then, this magician, he needed some volunteers, and —"

"Hey, Penny," she spoke to her sister, "what do you say we make like trees — and leave."

Ted couldn't believe what was happening. His mother and Cindy's suddenly began giggling helplessly, and simply turned and walked away from their *own* children!

"Ted! They don't know who we are," said Cindy, recovering somewhat. "We haven't been born yet. They aren't even married to our fathers. Those are the Whipple sisters, Penny and Molly, and they're just teenagers."

"Now that's the weirdest thing that's happened to us yet."

"*Sure* is," Cindy agreed.

"I never thought I'd live to see the day that I would start giving Mom some long, involved excuse and then see her giggle. Boy, I'm going to remember this day for a long time."

The cousins nodded to each other.

Just then, there was a bustle of noise and a loud burst of familiar chatter. The cage they were walking toward was filled with squirrel monkeys just like Sherlock.

Sherlock pushed his way out of the top of Cindy's backpack. He perched on her shoulder for just a second, as if to make sure he heard correctly. Suddenly, without warning, Sherlock made a dash for the monkey cage. He made his way through the crowd rapidly, jumping from shoulder to shoulder, leaving confused and angry people behind him.

Then, as Ted watched in horror, Sherlock landed squarely on the head of a young man. Sherlock startled the teenager so badly that he tossed his soda up into the air. The cold, sticky liquid landed squarely on Molly Whipple. When the young man turned to Molly to apologize, Ted saw his face for the first time. It was his father! Exactly like in the picture album at home.

Ted's father pulled a handkerchief from his

pocket and began apologizing profusely to Ted's mother. She was acting huffy and annoyed.

"Look, I'm really sorry, miss. I couldn't help it. Here, let me dry — no, maybe you'd better do it."

Ted's mother tried to wipe off the mess as his father kept apologizing, looking around for the real culprit.

Ted and Cindy had run over and fetched Sherlock. Ted's father's eyes lit on them with a look Ted knew well. It meant Trouble.

"Let's go!" Ted yelled to Cindy. They ran as fast as they could. They could hear heavy footsteps behind them. There was an open flap into the tent on their left. Without thinking further, they ducked into it.

They were in the clowns' dressing room and it was full of half-dressed and half-made-up clowns.

One clown stood in front of a full-length mirror, admiring his baggy pants, polka-dot shirt, and checked tie. He adjusted the brown fedora hat on his orange fright wig, and wiggled his

bulbous red nose to be sure it was secure.

Cindy and Ted brushed past the man and paused for a second in front of the mirror. Before the clown could give them a piece of his mind, they joined hands and stepped into the mirror.

A Stitch in Time

At first, they could barely hear the voice. But then it was louder and clearer.

"Ladies and gentlemen, boys and girls," they heard Kohoutek announce as they stepped onto the stage in the Exhibition Center Hall. They were standing in front of the antique mirror, but behind the magician's outspread cape. He dropped it to reveal them to the audience:

"Ted and Cindy, and their friend, Sherlock!!!" He paused for the roar of applause from the audience. "Brought back from the far side of the mirror by the Great Kohoutek!"

Ted and Cindy were astonished. They realized that they had only been gone a few seconds. Just the length of a magic trick. Yet, they'd traveled through three quarters of a century!

The audience continued to cheer as the stage lights went down. Kohoutek hustled them off into the wings.

"Why didn't you just tell us about the locket —" Cindy began.

"What locket?" Kohoutek said. "C'mon out and take a bow. You were terrific." He pulled them back onto the stage where they bowed to the roaring house as the stage lights came up.

When the curtain fell again, Kohoutek said, "Well, thanks again for being such able assistants." He started toward his dressing room.

"Just a minute," Ted said.

"Yes?" The magician turned and smiled at Ted and Cindy.

"We would have helped with the locket, and the instant picture that had to be inside it, without being tricked," Cindy declared.

"We sure would have," Ted added. "After all, if we hadn't been helping you, we never would have gotten to the circus. And if we hadn't gone to the circus, my parents might never have met — then where would *I* be?"

"Helped? Locket? Picture? Parents? What *are* you two talking about?" Kohoutek asked, smiling. "Here, here," he said as Sherlock jumped up into his arms and pulled loose a small piece of latex mask that had been stuck beneath his ear. "What's this?" he said, snatching the piece of disguise from Sherlock's hand.

"Okay, Kohoutek," Ted said. "If that's the way you want it." The cousins turned to leave.

Kohoutek strode after them so quickly that he bumped into Ted as he stopped, and turned Ted and Cindy toward himself.

"Ted, Cindy!" They studied him. "Don't you know that a magician never reveals the secrets of his illusions?" Ted nodded. "It had to be done," Kohoutek continued. "You were a great help, and I'm thankful. I hope you enjoy your souvenir. So, until we meet again...." Gracefully, Kohoutek bowed. "... and we will," he said, looking at them. Then, he winked.

With that, he whipped his cape over his shoulder and left them.

"Wait a minute," Ted exclaimed loudly, suddenly remembering that he had forgotten to return Kohoutek's watch. He reached into his back pocket where he had put the watch after taking it from Sherlock.

It was gone. In its place was a small oval photograph of Great-Granny Morehouse — just like the one in the locket. Ted smiled and showed Cindy the photograph Kohoutek had left them as a souvenir of their time travel.

The cousins stared after the magician for a moment and then turned to go home.

"Cindy," Ted said uncertainly, "I think we'd better not tell my parents about introducing them. Somehow, I don't think it would go over too well. Dad may still be angry about Sherlock and the soda. You never know. But what are we going to tell our families when they ask what happened to the locket?"

Cindy smiled wisely.

"I think we'll tell them we lost it — just in time!"

Clues to the Second Mystery

Enke	D'Arrest	Oort's Cloud
Brooke	Whipple	Shooting Star
Gale	Bennett	76
Biela	Harrington Abell	1910
Tuttle	Temple One	1066
Forbes	Sherlock (Holmes)	(141)
Finlay	Morehouse	989
Donati	Edmund	1986
Kohoutek	Bayeux	

- Astronomy Handbook
- "What is named for long hair, but has no hair at all?"
- "The heavens themselves blaze forth the death of princes."
- Captain of the *Paramour*
- Remonortsa layor d noces — Second Royal Astronomer, spelled backward.
- I Gameh t Fono Itaroda S'ottoig — Giotto's "Adoration of the Magi," spelled backward.
- Grotto Shinas — anagram for shooting star
- Publisher of Newton's book, *Principia Mathematica*
- "See You Later, Alligator" and "Rock Around the Clock"

Still don't know the answer?

Turn the Page

To solve this mystery, hold this page up to a mirror.

The solution to the second mystery is HALLEY'S COMET

The first 16 names in the listing on page 95 are all names of comets. The numbers in the listing are the dates when Halley's Comet appeared, at approximately **76** year intervals. (141) is 141 B.C. The word comet comes from the Greek words meaning **"long haired."**

Halley's Comet was named for **Edmund Halley**, who first predicted its return. Halley **published Newton's book, Principia Mathematica,** and as a young man was captain of the research ship, **Paramour.** Later he became Britain's **second Royal Astronomer.**

Halley's Comet was depicted by **Giotto** in his **"Adoration of the Magi,"** and by weavers of the **Bayeux** Tapestry, which recounts the Battle of Hastings in **1066.** Comets, unlike **shooting stars,** were thought to be bad omens, which is why Shakespeare has a character in Julius Caesar say: **"The heavens themselves blaze forth the death of princes."**

Nobody knows the origin of comets for sure, but one theory is that they come from a cluster outside our solar system knows as Oort's Cloud.

Finally, **"See You Later, Alligator,"** and **"Rock Around the Clock,"** are two old rock songs, recorded by none other than Bill Halley and the Comets.